Dreamland Fairies

Dreamland
Fairies

Written by
Nicola Baxter

Illustrated by
Beverlie Manson

ARMADILLO

This edition printed in 2007

© 2006 Bookmart Limited

ISBN 978-184322-406-8
3 5 7 9 10 8 6 4

Published by Armadillo Books
an imprint of
Bookmart Limited
Registered Number 2372865
Trading as Bookmart Limited
Blaby Road
Wigston
Leicester
LE18 4SE

Produced for Bookmart Limited by Nicola Baxter
PO Box 215
Framingham Earl
Norwich Norfolk NR14 7UR

Designer: Amanda Hawkes
Production designer: Amy Barton
Editor: Sally Delaney

Printed in Singapore

Contents

A Dream for Everyone

Imagine a place that is very, very far away—and very, very near at the same time. Imagine a place that is always busy, and always peaceful. Imagine a place that is everywhere, and nowhere. It's difficult, isn't it? And yet, you have been there yourself. It is called Dreamland.

It is easy to visit Dreamland. You won't need a car or a bus or a plane. But you mustn't try too hard to get there, or it will suddenly, silently disappear!

The Dreamland fairies live there all the time, of course. They work hard to bring you the dreams you want and the dreams you need. And to do their work well, they have to be really, really good at

dreaming!

Dreams are very special. They can take you anywhere you like and bring you safely home again in time for a brand new day. So how do the Dreamland fairies do their important work? Let me explain...

The best way to show you how dreams are made,
is to find someone who needs a dream right now.
Let's see. Far away from Dreamland, but very
near at the same time, the sun is just setting
behind a hill, and the sky is turning
from orange, to pink, to purple.

On the edge of a nearby wood,
someone needs a dream.
In fact, lots of someones
need dreams tonight.

Under the roots of an old
hawthorn tree, Mrs.
Matilda Rabbit is putting
her little ones to bed.
There are five of them!

Up in the branches above, Mr. Benjamin Bird is settling his three chicks down for the night.

By a little stream, running close by, Great Aunt Phoebe Frog is trying to persuade her lively great nephew to snuggle down in his bed of weeds and cool, comfy mud.

"Sweet dreams,
Chick One, Chick
Two, and Chick Three!"
coos Mr. Bird, as he pulls
a piece of moss around his
little ones. (Mr. Bird is
still thinking about names
for his nestlings.)

"Sweet dreams, Rodney,
Rosie, Rickie, Radish,
and Snoople!" calls Mrs.
Rabbit, as she closes the
bedroom door.

"Sweet
Dreams,
Glurgle!" croaks
Great Aunt Phoebe, and
pushes him firmly into the
squelchy mud.

10

And from the bedroom, and the nest, and the muddy, froggy bed, little dream-wishes rise up into the air. You can hardly see them but, like tiny bubbles, they drift up, up, up . . . and pop with a *ping!* in Dreamland.

Ping! A little fairy wakes, knowing at once that a very wet and weedy dream is needed for a sleepy froglet.

Ping! An older fairy understands that three little chicks want to share a dream tonight.

Ping! Ping! Ping! Ping! Ping! A group of fairy friends has a lot to do! Those wriggling rabbits have all got very different ideas about the dreams they need.

The dream for a froglet is not hard for even a small fairy
to organize. Fairy Rose flies off into Dreamland at once.
She soon comes to a big, beautiful lake, where
dragonflies hover above deep, cool water, and water lilies
bloom like stars across the shining surface.

Fairy Rose does not like swimming. She stands at the
edge of the lake and calls out in her silvery voice.
"Samuel! Are you there?"

Almost at once, a little
golden fish pops up his
head. "How can I help?"
he asks cheerfully.
"It's a dream for a
young frog, Sammy,"
Fairy Rose explains.

"You don't have to explain," groans the fish. "All frogs want to dream about is chasing fish like me. I've done this a dozen times. Just leave it to me. What's the name of the young fellow?"

Fairy Rose tells him and flies off with a wave and a happy smile. That was an easy job. She knows that Samuel will swim through Glurgle's dreams until morning, making the froglet happy and giving Great Aunt Phoebe the peaceful night she deserves.

Finding a dream for little birds to share is trickier, but Fairy Fern knows that those little birds are nearly ready to fly. An exciting flying dream is just what they need.

Fairy Fern goes to see a butterfly friend. "I need a dream for three birds to share," she explains. "I'd like some gentle flying to put them in the mood for their father's lessons tomorrow. I know he is worried."

"Then perhaps you should be finding a dream for him!" the butterfly laughs. "I'm sorry, I can't help you tonight. I have already agreed to appear in a bunny's dream."

A dragonfly sighs sadly. "No, I'm resting my wings tonight, I'm afraid." Several little birds are also already busy. "You could ask the hawk," they chirp.

Fairy Fern is afraid the hawk will frighten Mr. Bird's little ones. She is upset that she can't find a flying friend to help. Then one of the little birds she has asked flies after her. "Why don't you do it yourself, Fairy Fern? You can fly!"

The little fairy laughs, and all night long, in the little birds' dreams, she flutters and flaps, whizzes and zooms, so that they just can't wait to fly themselves.

Now for those sleeping bunnies. They are all such different
little bunnies that they all want different kinds of dreams.
And bunnies are impatient. That's why they bounce
around so much. It's no good waiting until the sun is
slipping up into the sky again before they each have a good
dream. Three fairy friends have some quick thinking to do.

Fairy Bluebell closes her eyes to concentrate on the dream
wishes floating up towards her. "Rodney Rabbit wants to
dream about pirates," she says, "and Rosie Rabbit
would love to be a ballerina. Rickie and Radish are very
keen on jumping. They want to be winners in the Rabbit
Olympics. As for Snoople, I don't understand
what he wants to dream about at all!"

Fairy Mallow closes her eyes, too. "You're right," she says. "I don't understand a thing that is going on in that young bunny's head. He can't really be wanting to dream about dust, can he?"

"Nobody wants to dream about dust," giggles Fairy Lime. "Let me try." She closes her eyes and laughs. "He doesn't want to dream about dust," she says. "He has tumbled out of bed and crawled underneath it. The dust under the bed is tickling his nose and … oh, dear … he has sneezed and woken up all his brothers and sisters. Poor Mrs. Rabbit is settling them down again."

While a frazzled rabbit mother persuades her babies to go back to sleep, the fairies set to work. Fairy Bluebell doesn't much like flying over the Dreamland sea in search of pirates, but she is lucky to find Captain Thunder-thump, the most famous pirate of them all, on dry land. He is dealing with the woodworm in his leg.

"Captain, would you have time for a quick bit of swash-buckling this evening?" she asks. "I know a young rabbit who would love to meet you."

The pirate shakes his fist as the last woodworm crawls away and nods his head. "I haven't anything better to do tonight," he says. "Do you mind if I bring my friend Blood-thirsty Battling Bertha?"

18

"Not at all," agrees Fairy Bluebell. "I don't suppose she does ballet dancing, does she?"

Bloodthirsty Battling Bertha strides into the room at just that moment. It doesn't look as if she owns a tutu. Fairy Bluebell hopes her friends are having better luck.

Meanwhile, Fairy Mallow has tried to persuade several kangaroos, a couple of grasshoppers and whole families of frogs to help with a dream for Rickie and Radish. All are already busy. With the Rabbit Olympics so soon, Rickie and his brother are not the only two rabbits keen on jumping.

"There's only one answer," sighs Mallow, "but Mrs. Rabbit isn't going to like it."

Fairy Lime finds not one bunny ballerina but a whole company looking for an audience. And since Snoople now seems to want a very noisy dream, she brings along the whole orchestra, too.

Five little bunnies spend a very happy night, but Fairy Mallow is right about Mrs. Rabbit. When she hears that Rickie and Radish have spent several hours dreaming about athletic fleas, she is very cross. "I shall write a letter to the Dreamland Council," she says. "What kind of a dream is that to give young, impressionable rabbits?"

As for the Dreamland fairies, their work is far from done. For them, as dreamers in one part of the world are waking up, sleepy little ones across the ocean are settling down to sleep … and dream, of course.

A Dream
for
Dragons

On a perfect pink cloud in Dreamland, Fairy Snowflake
is dreaming of frosty forests and sparkling streams, when
she is suddenly woken by a dream wish that pops near
her ear with a little puff of smoke!

"Oh," cries Snowflake, "this dream wish feels hot!
I don't like it at all!"

She closes her eyes to
concentrate on what the
dreamer needs, then
quickly opens them
again in surprise.
The sleepy wish
is from a dragon!

"I can't find a dream for a dragon!" cries the fairy. "I don't know where to start!" She even tries (and Dreamland fairies really are not supposed to do this) to pretend she hasn't received the wish. But a dragon's wishes are very fierce. More and more dream wishes float up towards her, each hotter and more urgent than the one before.

"Help! I need the Dreamland Council!" cries the fairy. And she flies off at once to find the cloud where the council meets.

Fairy Snowflake is so nervous, standing before the wise fairies and elves of the Dreamland Council that her words come out in little scattered flurries, like snow.

"Slowly, slowly, my dear," says a kind old wizard. "You will need to tell us all about the dreamer before we can help you to find a dream."

The Snowflake Fairy closes her eyes and concentrates. "Oh, I don't like it!" she cries. "There are three dragons. They live in … in a cave under a volcano. Oh!"

"What is it?" asks the wizard. "Don't be afraid. Dream wishes cannot hurt you. Just tell us clearly."

Fairy Snowflake is not happy. "They want horrible dreams!" she says. "I can't do this! Oh, help me!"

The kindly wizard smiles. "I can feel these dream wishes, too," he says. "You know, these are just the kinds of dreams that dragons like to have. You love to dream of cool, white snow and frosty air. Dragons love treasure and adventure and fire! There is nothing for you to fear. I have an idea. Come with me."

"My name is Greybeard," the wizard explains. "I am going to take you to see a friend of mine. I'm afraid I can't fly like you, so we'll have to travel by magic carpet. I hope you don't mind. It's old-fashioned, I know, but sometimes the old ways are the best."

Snowflake nods vaguely. She has no idea what a magic carpet is. The next instant, she finds herself sitting on a rug that is hovering in space. It looks very old. Snowflake is pretty sure she sees a moth fluttering out of it. She also thinks it is a little bit, well, *smelly*.

Wizard Greybeard settles down happily beside her. "This is the only way to travel!" he cries. "Now I need to concentrate for a moment." He shuts his eyes and starts to mumble. Snowflake wonders if he has fallen asleep.

Suddenly, the rug gives a terrifying lurch and shoots off at incredible speed through Dreamland. Snowflake screams. "I'm going to fall! Help!"

"It only feels like that," cries Wizard Greybeard. "The carpet would never let you fall off. Smile, my dear. You'll soon start to enjoy the ride."

But before Snowflake has a chance to enjoy anything, the rug screeches to a stop as suddenly as it started. It is hovering outside the window of a large, dilapidated and rather blackened castle. The owner is at home!

Well, several unfortunate things happen all at once. Snowflake screams at the sight of the dragon. The dragon rears back in shock and hits his head on the edge of the window. In pain, he lets out a bellow of his own, and with it comes a fierce rush of flames. Wizard Greybeard yells, "Help! My carpet is on fire!" and quickly says a spell for rain.

It feels as if someone very large has thrown a bucket of water from a high window. Snowflake and the wizard land on the ground … soaked!

Whoosh!

"I could blow on you gently to dry you out," says a voice from above. "No!" cry two voices. For the first time, Fairy Snowflake and Wizard Greybeard are thinking the same thing.

The dragon appears in a nearby doorway. "I won't even breathe, I promise!" he says, and he looks so sorry that even Snowflake smiles. "I'm afraid we haven't made a very good start," says the dragon. "My name is Ashe. How can I help you?"

"Well, we came because my friend here is frightened of dragons," says the wizard. "This was perhaps not my best ever idea!" Suddenly, with a spluttering and snorting, he begins to laugh. It isn't long before Snowflake and Ashe are laughing, too. And it just shows what a very nice dragon he is that not even a whiff of steam comes from his mouth and nose.

Together, Fairy Snowflake and Wizard Greybeard explain about the dragon dream.

"Well, of course, I know exactly what they want to dream about," says Ashe. "Treasure and adventure and frightening a few knights and their pages. Would you like me to sort this out for you?"

"Would you?" gasps Snowflake.

"Could you?" asks Greybeard. "No real fighting, mind, and no one must get hurt. I know what you dragons are like when you start dreaming."

"I promise," says Ashe in a little voice, looking like a naughty puppy. "Well, I must make a start."

Extraordinarily gracefully, he rises into the air. "We must set off for home," says Greybeard, then looks doubtfully at the singed carpet.

"I could give you a lift!" calls the dragon.

So that is how a snowflake fairy has two exciting flights in one night, without flapping her own wings at all. And three dragons under a volcano have the best dreams of their lives without hurting anyone.

A Dream
for
Mermaids

Deep beneath the sea is a wonderful world where bright little fishes swish and swirl, seaweed sways with the tide, and mermaids comb their hair in the blue waters.

It is a dreamy world, so perhaps you think that the kinds of dreams we have are not needed. That's not true. Even octopuses dream, and mermaids are the greatest dreamers of all, as this story shows.

One sleepy afternoon, a water fairy is resting on a raincloud when a dream bubble pops near her ear and out jumps a little fish! Water fairies do not have wings, but they can dive through the air and sea like birds. The water fairy picks up the fish and dives gracefully into the water far below.

With a smile, the water fairy lets the little fish swim off through the clear, blue water. "Now," she wonders, "where is the mermaid who sent that dream wish?"

The water fairy, whose name is Marina, swims gently through the water, enjoying the beautiful scene. Then, behind a rock, she sees a stream of yellow hair rippling in the current. A mermaid is sitting there.

Now dream fairies do not usually make themselves known to the people and animals whose dreams they are helping to create. You haven't ever met *your* dream fairy, have you? But Marina is looking worried. She can tell, even without seeing her face, that the mermaid behind the rock is crying.

Dream fairies are very good at sensing another person's feelings—that's why they are so good at finding just the right dream. It wouldn't be easy for you or me to tell if a mermaid is crying. You can't see tears underwater. But Marina knows, and she hates to see such unhappiness.

Marina can't help herself. She swims over to the mermaid and asks, "My dear, are you all right?"

The mermaid looks up with a face that would melt the heart of a hungry shark. "I miss them so," she sobs. "I miss my family." And she is so upset that her tears fall as pearls onto the sandy seabed.

"Where is your family?" asks Marina gently, trying not to let the mermaid see her too clearly.

The mermaid sighs. "They are on the other side of the southern ocean," she says. "I agreed to come here to serve the mer-queen, and my parents and sisters were so proud that I was chosen, but I miss them terribly. I cannot let them know, though. They would be so disappointed in me."

"Certainly, they would be sorry to know that you were unhappy," Marina agrees. "You send them messages, I suppose?"

"Oh yes," says the mermaid. "I send messages by all the little fish who pass, but I try to sound happy, and it is not the same as seeing their lovely faces again."

"Of course not!" Marina is already beginning to have an idea, but she needs to consult the Dream Council before she can go ahead with her plan. She gently says goodbye to the mermaid and swims up towards the surface.

It is only when she has disappeared from view that the mermaid suddenly realizes that the kind stranger did not have a tail!

Out in the open air again, Marina soars upward to the clouds where the Dream Council meets.

A fairy greets her as she arrives. "How can we help you, water fairy?"

"I wish," says Marina slowly, "at least, I should like, well…" The fairy urges her on with a smile. "I want," Marina says in a rush, "to do something that is not allowed!"

"You had better come and tell us all about it," says the fairy gravely. Marina fears that she looks a little shocked.

A few minutes later, having heard Marina's story, the wise fairies and wizards of the Dream Council are looking calmly at her.

"You know," says one, "that we have our rules for a reason. You cannot send a dream to someone unless they have asked for it. Human beings often do not know themselves well enough to realize that they have asked for a dream, so their dreams are often surprises for them, but it is different with mermaids. Only the mermaid you met has asked for a dream. You cannot send dreams to her family as well."

Marina hangs her head. "But it would make them all so happy," she says. "If they cannot be together in their daily lives, surely they can be together in their dreams."

The members of the Dream Council look at each other. "We need some time to discuss this," they say. "Could you wait on that cloud over there?"

Marina feels a little spark of hope warming her. She had expected the Council simply to say no. It is agony waiting on the cloud, so she tries to pass the time by counting the dream bubbles that float up beside her.

At last, the friendly fairy Marina met when she arrived flutters over. "The Council is ready to talk to you now," she says.

An old wizard speaks for everyone else. "Well, you have given us an interesting problem," he says. "Dreams are very special things. We still do not think that you can send a dream to someone who has not asked for it. Still, we like your idea, so there is only one answer. You will have to make sure the other mermaids far across the sea *do* ask to dream about the mer- queen's maid."

"However am I going to do that?" asks Marina, but the wizard smiles. "Ah, that is your problem, not ours, my dear. Good luck!"

Marina swoops back to the ocean. She has no idea what to do next, but she knows that talking to her friends is often helpful when she cannot think what to do. She finds them playing with a dolphin near a small island. They listen carefully to what she has to say.

"The mermaid's family must have dreams, too," says Pearl, another water fairy. "But there is only one way you can find out. You will have to travel to the other side of the southern ocean to find out what kind of dreams they like."

"But it is far! Very, very far!" cries Marina. "I don't think that I can go so far."

Suddenly there is a *whoosh* of water, as the friendly dolphin jumps and spins beside her. "I will take you," he says. "Just climb on!"

So that is just what Marina does. "What an adventure!" she calls to the dolphin, but the sea is rushing by so quickly that he cannot hear her.

A long time later—but not as long as Marina imagined—the fairy and her friend arrive at a beautiful coral reef. Sitting on rocks, combing their hair and talking quietly together, are several mer-people.

They are so deep in conversation that they do not see Marina arrive. She cannot help overhearing them.

"It was right that she should go to the mer-queen," says one. "We could not hold her back. But I miss her so much I hardly know what to do."

"I know," says another. "Her messages sound so happy. I don't like to tell her we wish she was back here with us."

Marina can hardly believe her ears. All the time the little mermaid has been missing her family, her family has been missing *her*!

The water fairy glides into view and hovers in front of the mer-people. "Forgive me for interrupting you," she says, "but I heard what you said—couldn't you visit your relative?"

"Oh, it is too far," sighs a mermaid.
"We have work to do here."

"I didn't mean swimming there," Marina explains. "You could visit her in your dreams." Then she swims quickly away, fearing that she has said too much.

That night, as stars twinkle over the glittering ocean, Marina sits on a cloud near the moon and waits. Suddenly, lots of little dream bubbles swirl around her as if they are dancing. They are from mer-people, wanting to dream about other mer-people, and Marina is pretty sure she knows exactly where they have come from. With a smile and a sigh of happiness, she gets to work. It is going to be a very busy night!

A Dream for Unicorns

Fairies live for a very, very long time. Fairy Serena is not an old fairy by any means, but she has lived for hundreds of years and helped with many, many dreams.

Nothing much surprises her these days—not rabbits asking for dreams about tap-dancing foxes, not butterflies asking for dreams about giants, not even giants asking for dreams about butterflies! But one moonlit night, as she rests comfortably on a cloud in Dreamland, Serena is very surprised indeed.

As a silvery dream bubble pops beside her, Serena sits up and says "Oh!" And then she wonders if she herself is dreaming, because the dream request that has just popped into her head is so very strange.

Serena flies around her cloud, feeling the breeze on her face and the warmth of the sun on her wings. No, she is not dreaming. She really has been asked for a dream by a unicorn!

Now you may wonder why this is odd. If rabbits can have dreams, and dragons can have dreams, and every creature that ever appeared in a storybook can have dreams, why can't a unicorn?

Well, what you may not know, but fairies know very well, is that unicorns never ever sleep. They are the most magical creatures of all, more magical even than fairies. Their magic is so powerful that they cannot sleep even if they try. Imagine a fizzy drink, full of bubbles. Those bubbles are like a unicorn's magic. They are always moving, popping, fizzing and if they ever stop—well, then it isn't a fizzy drink any more.

It's the same with unicorns. A unicorn without magic simply cannot exist.

So how can a unicorn possibly need a dream?

Fairy Serena flies thoughtfully off to find her friend Starlight. The nighttime fairy is not resting or dreaming. She is sitting bolt upright on her cloud with a look of great surprise on her face.

"You'll never guess what has just happened!" she tells Serena in amazement.

But Serena has guessed already. Have you? "You've just had a dream request from a unicorn," she says. "Am I right?"

Serena and Starlight talk over what has happened.

"It's impossible," says Starlight. "Unicorns never sleep. I know that some creatures have daydreams, but those are not the same as the dreams that Dreamland fairies arrange. What can it mean?"

"If only we could ask them!" says Serena. "But we are not allowed to talk directly to dreamers. We will simply have to go down to the Forest of Enchantment and see if we can find out. It will be difficult though. Unicorns know when any other magical creature is near."

That gives Starlight an idea. "Come with me!" she cries, swooping away across the sky. "I know someone who can help us!"

Before long, the two fairies are flying through a very different sky, where dark grey and purple clouds are gathered, and only a few fairies can be seen peeping from the shadows.

"But this is the place where bad dreams come!" cries Serena. She feels a little frightened, although she knows there is no need.

Please do not think that bad dreams and nightmares ever come from Dreamland. They do not. But Dreamland fairies can sometimes help to put right a dream that has become frightening or sad. They work hard to make sure that all dreams have happy endings. It is hard work, and Serena admires the fairies who do this. But why has her friend brought her here?

Starlight flies straight up to a beautiful fairy dressed in purple and silver.

"Starlight! How lovely to see you!" cries the fairy. "But why are you here?"

Starlight turns to Serena. "This is my friend Twilight," she explains. "She can help us to visit the unicorns without being seen."

"Ah," Twilight smiles. "You want to borrow a Cloud of Darkness."

Serena has no idea what this means, but she soon finds out. Clouds of Darkness are not really clouds at all. In fact, sometimes you can't even see them. But they hide things really well. They are like a kind of invisible mist. Have you ever not been able to find something that was right under your nose? Maybe a little Cloud of Darkness was hovering nearby for a moment!

A few minutes later, Serena and Starlight float off on their special cloud towards the Forest of Enchantment.

The forest is a truly wonderful place. Parts of it are shadowy and secret, with magical stars glittering among the trees.

53

Other parts seem to be lit by sunlight all the time, as if the trees themselves are glowing. Everywhere there are bright little flowers and butterflies.

The trees are magical, too. Some of them grow jewels, glinting and sparkling. Others sing as you pass by. Some bend down and stroke you gently with their branches. Many whisper your name when you are near.

Serena and Starlight hover through the forest on their cloud. It is like a magic carpet in a way. The fairies can see each other, and all the birds and animals above can see them clearly, but from underneath the cloud makes them invisible.

"There are some unicorns! Look!" whispers Serena.

54

Sure enough a little group of the magical horses is standing in a clearing.

The fairies close their eyes so that they can hear what they are "saying". Unicorns do not actually speak, they listen to each other's thoughts. As fairies are magical, too, they can hear these thoughts if they concentrate really hard. That is why closing their eyes helps.

In a very short time, Serena and Starlight know exactly why the unicorns are asking for dreams. They fly quickly away to talk about what to do next.

"This is terrible," says Serena. "I had no idea."

You see, the unicorns need dreams because they are beginning to sleep. And they are beginning to sleep because their magical powers are fading away. Why is this happening? It is happening because children, who are almost as magical as fairies, have stopped believing in unicorns.

"There must be something we can do," gasps Serena. "This can't go on. If unicorns lose all their magic, they simply disappear. Soon there will be no unicorns at all."

Starlight nods. "This is happening because unicorns are such clever, secretive creatures," she says. "They are very good at remaining hidden. Children sometimes catch just the tiniest glimpse of a fairy, so they still believe in us, but they hardly ever see even the smallest part of a unicorn."

"Perhaps we can change that," says Serena slowly. "Are you thinking what I'm thinking?"

"You mean we could give children dreams about unicorns?" whispers Starlight. "That's an excellent idea. But, you know, we can only give dreams that are asked for. Children almost never ask for dreams about unicorns."

"That's true," Serena agrees, "but there are lots of children who wish for a dream but are not sure what they want to dream about. We could send all of them unicorn dreams."

"It is too much work for the two of us…," Starlight begins.

"Of course! We need all our friends to help!" cries Serena. "Hurry! There's no time to lose!"

So that night, fairies all over Dreamland send unicorn dreams to children everywhere. Perhaps you have had one yourself!

Meanwhile, Serena and Starlight remember that they each have a dream request to fulfil. To the unicorns they send dreams of magical hope and happiness, to help them until their own magic returns.

It is not long before children all over the world are talking about unicorns.

Some of them do not remember their dreams and wonder why unicorns have popped into their heads. All of them agree that unicorns are the most wonderful magical creatures of all. And you will be pleased to know that from that night to this, not a single Dreamland fairy has received a dream request from a unicorn.

"I love to be asked for dreams," Serena tells her friend Starlight, "but this is one time when I'm very, very glad to have no requests at all— well only from lots of children wanting dreams about unicorns, anyway!"

A Dream for a Wizard

One quiet evening, the Dreamland fairies are sitting on their clouds, watching the sky turn pink and gold and purple as the day comes to an end. Soon, they know, pretty dream bubbles will start to rise as sleepy little ones everywhere begin to close their eyes.

60

"I love this time of day," says Fairy Marigold. "It's exciting, not knowing what kind of dream requests are going to come. We never know what will happen next. That's what I love about Dreamland."

A second later, Marigold's words come true—but not in the way she meant! There is a puff of purple smoke and a silvery ringing sound. The fairies look around in surprise. Only an older fairy, Emmelina, begins to smile. "Little ones," she says, "I think we are about to have a visitor."

There is another puff of smoke. The silvery ringing becomes louder and begins to sound slightly out of tune. One or two of the fairies' clouds begin to shake and bob about in the sky.

"Whatever is happening?" cries Marigold.

"No need to worry!" replies a deep, quavery voice. "It's only me!" And all at once a strange-looking fellow in a tall hat and a cloak lands with a bump on Marigold's cloud! His long stockinged legs wave in the air as he tries to regain his balance. "I'm so sorry," he says. "My landings are getting worse and worse. Perhaps I need to retake my flying test."

Marigold hardly knows what to say, she is so surprised. But Emmelina flies over and helps the old man to sit up and straighten his hat and cloak.

"I believe I have the pleasure of greeting Wizard Moonbeam," she smiles. "You visited once when I was a very young fairy, sir, and I have always remembered you."

"Well, that is very kind of you. Very kind indeed," says the wizard. "Yes, it is some while since I was here. I felt it was time for me to visit again. I am sure that everything is in order."

Seeing the confused looks on some fairy faces, Emmelina explains. "Wizard Moonbeam comes to Dreamland every so often as an inspector," she says. "He makes sure that we are making happy dreams and that all our dreamers are pleased with them. I hope you have had no complaints, sir, since you were here last?"

"Well, not really," says the wizard. "Those pixies who live in the Higgledy Hills are always muttering and moaning, you know. It's not your fault, my dears. They are simply too silly most of the time to ask for the dreams they really want. If they will fall asleep thinking about apple pies and red nightcaps, then that is what they will dream about."

"Last week one of them wanted to dream about a pair of slippers," laughs a little fairy.

"I know," smiles the wizard. "Someone should teach those pixies how to ask for dreams properly. I suppose I will have to go over there myself one day. Now, I must get back to business."

"What would you like to see while you are here?" Emmelina asks the visitor. "Dream wishes will begin to arrive at any moment, so we shall soon be busy."

"Of course, of course," says the wizard, "and that is just as it should be. With your permission I will simply sit here and observe." Seeing the confused looks of some of the smallest fairies, he explains, "That just means that I will watch what you do and give advice if I think you need it."

No sooner has the wizard finished speaking than two or three dream bubbles float up beside the fairies.

Wizard Moonbeam watches as each dream bubble bursts
with a *ping!* beside a little fairy. "I never know," he says
with a smile, "if the bubble somehow chooses a fairy or if
it is just chance who is nearby when it bursts."

One little fairy laughs excitedly. "A little elf wants a dream
about a princess," she says. "I'm off to see Princess
Corona. She is always *so* kind. And her palace is lovely!"

"Quite right, my dear," says Wizard Moonbeam.
"A very good choice."

Another little fairy looks puzzled. "A seagull wants a dream about fish," she says. "I don't really know what to do."

"Yes, you do," says Emmelina kindly. "Where do fish live? In the sea! And who can help you there?"

"Oh, a water fairy!" cries the little one. "Of course! That's easy!" And she flies off towards the ocean.

"Well, everything seems to be going very well here," says the wizard. "I think you hardly need to be inspected. But, oh dear me, whatever is the matter over there?"

On a large cloud nearby, a little fairy dressed in golden yellow is sobbing as if her heart will break.

67

Emmelina hurries over to help her, but the little fairy just cries harder when she sees her.

"I'm so sorry," she sobs. "I know I shouldn't have done it!"

Emmelina glances at Wizard Moonbeam. "Done what?" she asks in the gentlest voice you can imagine.

"I … I … I refused a dream request!" says the fairy. "It all happened so quickly. I didn't really mean to. It was just so silly, that's all. And I wanted to arrange a beautiful dream, so that you would be proud of me!"

Now it is an important rule in Dreamland that no dream request, no matter what it is, can be ignored. Sometimes dreams need to be changed a little bit to make them just right, but it is not the fairies' job to say whether a dream can be delivered or not. If there is any question, the Dreamland Council must be consulted.

Wizard Moonbeam cannot help looking shocked, but his voice is not unkind when he speaks. "What exactly was the dream request?" he asks.

69

"It was from a pixie," sobs the little fairy. Emmelina and the wizard exchange a look of understanding. "He wanted a dream about Toffo-licious-munchy-crunchies."

"About *what*?" exclaims the wizard.

"Toffo-licious-munchy-crunchies," says Emmelina. "They are a new pixie breakfast cereal. Everyone—at least—everyone who's a pixie—is talking about them."

"It certainly is a very silly thing to want to dream about," says the wizard, "but as you know, my dear, that is not for us to decide. Now, I think we are going to have to go to the Higgledy Hills to sort this matter out. And I can have a

few words with those tricky pixies while we are there. You had better come too, little one. What is your name?"

"B-Buttercup," stammers the poor fairy. "I'll never do anything like this again. I promise!"

"I hope not," says the wizard, but his eyes are twinkling. "Now, can we fly to the Higgledy Hills on a cloud? My flying isn't always very reliable these days."

Emmelina soon summons up a suitable cloud, and the three set out. The Higgledy Hills, like so many things in Dreamland, are a long way away in the daytime but very close by when your eyes are shut. Only a minute or two later, the cloud hovers among the hills.

It is daytime in the Higgledy Hills, not bedtime as the fairies have imagined. Buttercup is able to lead the others to a little red doorway in a hillside. "He lives in here," she whispers.

Wizard Moonbeam knocks loudly on the door. Almost at once, it creaks open. A pixie mother is standing there, looking upset and worried.

"Excuse me, madam," says the wizard. "My name is Moonbeam. I believe your son may be having trouble sleeping."

The pixie looks surprised. "I wish he was," she says. "He sleeps all the time! Are you some kind of doctor? You'd better come in."

Inside, the little house is tidy and snug, like most pixie homes. The fairies, who think of pixies as naughty, difficult creatures, begin to feel that they may have been mistaken, especially when the pixie mother shows them to comfortable chairs and brings them nettle tea and cakes.

"I've been worried about young Ruffles for some time," she confesses, when she sits down herself at last. "He does nothing but sleep all day and all night. I have to wake him for mealtimes. Mind you, he seems perfectly happy and well when he is awake.

Just at that moment, a small pixie appears in the doorway. "I'm feeling a bit hungry," he says, yawning.

"Ruffles!" cries his mother. "You're awake! That's amazing!" She turns to the wizard. "Thank you, sir. And you didn't even have to see him! You must be a very clever doctor indeed."

"My dear woman, I haven't done anything," says the wizard. "I believe that my young assistant Buttercup here has done the trick. How are you feeling, young fellow?"

Ruffles scratches his nose and shrugs. "I'm fine," he says. "I don't feel like sleeping any more, that's all. In fact, I'd rather go out to play."

His mother is beaming. "That's wonderful!" she cries. "Play as long as you like, sweetheart. I'm sure your friends are down by the stream with their leaf-boats."

Ruffles hurries off at once, grabbing a cake as he goes. His mother is almost in tears. "I'm just so grateful," she says. "I've been so worried, but I didn't know what to do."

"There is nothing to worry about at all," the wizard reassures her, "but I will be giving a course of lectures in the next few weeks on the subject of sleeping and dreams. Perhaps you will bring your son along. I think that many pixies could learn something useful. But for now, we must be going."

Wizard Moonbeam and the fairies fly home on their cloud. The wizard smiles kindly at Buttercup. "I shall be giving a few lectures in Dreamland, as well," he says. "It's not that you are doing a bad job, my dears. You are doing too good a job! That young pixie had such wonderful dreams, supplied by you and your friends, that he never wanted to wake up! It was only when you drew the line at a dream about Toffo-licious-munchy-crunchies, my dear, that he decided being awake was more interesting! It's all a question of balance, you see. Well, you must come to my talk to find out."

Fairy Buttercup is so happy that she has not hurt anyone after all that she cannot help smiling. Emmelina also feels relieved. She hates to see an unhappy fairy. As soon as the cloud arrives back in Dreamland, the two fairies are eager to tell their friends what has happened. They turn to thank the wizard one more time, but he has fallen fast asleep on the comfortable, fluffy cloud!

"Poor Wizard Moonbeam! It's been a busy day for him," says Emmelina. Suddenly a little dream bubble bursts with a *ping!* near her ear. It is a dream request from a sleepy wizard!

Emmelina can't help laughing. "I think you need to help me with this one, Buttercup!" she giggles. "You seem to know more about it than I do. Wizard Moonbeam would like a dream, please, and I don't think we should say no."

"What does he want to dream about?" asks Buttercup. Then seeing Emmelina's face, she guesses all by herself, and one clever, tired wizard is soon deep in a delicious dream about … Toffo-licious-munchy-crunchies.

A Dream
for
You

Dreamland fairies are
busy—but they are never,
ever too busy to visit *you*.
When you are snuggled in
your bed, or drifting off to
sleep on a long journey,
somewhere far away (but,
as you know, very near as
well) Dreamland fairies
are waiting.

How do you ask for a
special dream? It's easy.
First you must be feeling
comfortable (*not*, really *not*
riding your bike or
crossing the road or doing
anything at all *dangerous*).
Now close your eyes.

No! Not actually *now*! You need to be able to read this book! In a minute, when you've finished, you can close your eyes. Then you need to think about something you long to dream about. It could be anything. Start imagining how your perfect dream would begin. Remember, in dreams you can go anywhere. You can be anyone. You can do anything you want to do. Dreams are your own private world, and no Dreamland fairy will ever tell another human being what you dream about. It is an important part of the Dreamland Law.

The stories in this book take a little while to read, but fairy time is not the same as human time. In these stories it sometimes takes a Dreamland fairy a long time to find the right dream, but years and years of fairy time are just a second to us. So before you have imagined even a minute or two of your perfect dream, the fairies will be at work, bringing you the dream you long for.

Does it always work? I think so, but sometimes it's really difficult to remember your dreams afterwards. They seem confused and strange. Trust the Dreamland fairies to bring you what you need, and remember, no one and nothing can ever harm you in a Dreamland dream. It simply wraps you safely in your own special story and carries you through to morning.